The Arrival

To Marie Reichman,
Blast off with the
Pond Punkies!
web fans,
Lisa Riehle
10-25-09

Larissa

Larissan Clan
Power: Fire
Eyes: Red
Hair: Red

Proteus

Proteusan Clan
Power: Shape Shifting
Eyes: Brown
Hair: Brown

Triton

Tritonan Clan
Power: Freeze
Eyes: White
Hair: White

Nereid

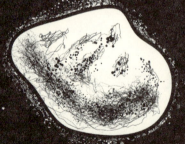

Nereidan Clan
Power: Invisibility
Eyes: Silver
Hair: Silver

POND PUNKIES® Universe

Neptune

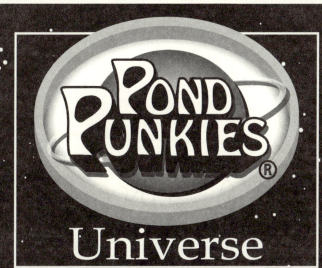

Naiad
Naiadan Clan
Power: Control Water
Eyes: Blue
Hair: Blue

N.T.A.
Neptune Training Academy

Unknown Zone

Galatea
Galatean Clan
Power: X-ray Vision
Eyes: Black
Hair: Black

Despina
Despinan Clan
Power: Stretch
Eyes: Green
Hair: Green

Thalassa
Thalassan Clan
Power: Read Minds
Eyes: Yellow
Hair: Yellow

Book One
The Arrival

Lisa Riebe
Cynthia Nunn
Illustrated by Eric Scott Fisher

RAVINE PUBLISHING
Morris, Illinois

Bang Printing certifies that this book complies with the specified rules, bans, standards and regulations enforced by the U.S. Consumer Product Safety Commission.

For information address
Ravine Publishing LLC
100 W. Commercial, Suite 1C #158
Morris, IL 60450

Educators and Librarians, for a variety of teaching tools, visit us at
www.pondpunkies.com

Publisher's Cataloging-in-Publication
(Provided by Quality Books, Inc.)

Riebe, Lisa
Pond punkies. Book one, The arrival / Lisa Riebe, Cynthia Nunn ; illustrated by Eric Scott Fisher.
p. cm.
SUMMARY: Blaze, an eleven-year-old Pond Punkie from Neptune is blasted to Earth where he must solve a prophecy to save Earth and Neptune.
Audience: Ages 7-11.
ISBN-13: 9780981949338
ISBN-10: 0981949339

1. Life on other planets--Juvenile fiction. 2. Ponds --Juvenile fiction. 3. Neptune (Planet)--Juvenile fiction. 4. Science fiction. [1. Life on other planets --Fiction. 2. Extraterrestrial beings--Fiction. 3. Ponds--Fiction. 4. Prophecies--Fiction. 5. Neptune (Planet)--Fiction. 6. Fantasy--Fiction. 7. Science fiction.] I. Nunn, Cynthia II. Fisher, Eric Scott III. Title. IV. Title: Arrival

PZ7.R42755Pon 2009   [E]
QBI09-700011

Printed in the United States of America
Bang Printing
Brainerd, Minnesota
March 2009

First Edition

For God, Greg, Justin, Joshua, mom, Bonnie B., and Sue,
true supporters of all my dreams.

For all the children who take time to read.

Many thanks to Phyllis Worland,
you rock!
L. R.
Mark 11:22-24

For Dave, Paul, Brittany, mom, dad and Diane.
C. N.

For Molly.
E. S. F.

Contents

CHAPTER ONE

The Unknown Zone

I crouched behind the frozen green wall surrounding the academy. Prickly plants clung to the sides of it. "You better get down lower, Ace," I said. "Those blue spikes you call hair may be standing a bit too tall tonight." The last thing we needed was to get caught sneaking out of the training academy by an Elder on the day before graduation.

Ace shot back, "Come on Blaze, your red hair is lit up like a fireball." He patted the top of his spikes, crawling past me on the bumpy frozen surface of Neptune, and said, "I just need to get some more gooey stuff. I can't leave Neptune without my secret ingredient for the gel. Did you bring that extra tube?"

"Yeah, I got it. Now keep your voice down and stay low," I said.

Ace ran his webbed hands upward through his hair like two moon rakes. He flashed me a grin, showing that all to familiar smile he used on the Elders, and said, "Soon Blaze, you will see my punkie gel on punkie heads everywhere, including Larissa." Even though Ace was a Pond Punkie from the Naiadan (Ni-ad-an) Clan, whose power is controlling water, and I'm a Pond Punkie from the Larissan (La-Riss-an) Clan with the power of fire, we were closer than any two stars in the Milky Way.

On our first moon orbit at the academy, where all eight Pond Punkie Clans go for training, the Elders paired Ace and me together. At training, they caught us listening in on one of their meetings. We have been best friends since that night. We were only eight moon orbits old. Now, three moon orbits later, we have control of our powers and understand how they will help Earth.

If the Elders knew we were leaving the academy grounds, we would be in big trouble. The Elders were the older Pond Punkies who instructed us at N.T.A. Neptune Training Academy. The academy was a huge fortress sitting smack in the middle of Neptune's bright side. Ace and I called it Nereid's Torture Academy. Nereid was the meanest, cruelest, and ugliest Elder ever to step a webbed foot on Neptune.

I stopped at the large locked gate guarding the academy entrance and said, "Ace I'm not so sure about this."

Ace punched me in the arm and said, "Come on, dude. This is my last chance to get the gel."

I thought about it for an instant, punched him back and said, "What are friends for." I turned toward the gate. "Uh-oh," I said. Nereid crept up behind Ace.

"What?" asked Ace.

Before I could answer, Nereid grabbed Ace's arm and reached for my neck. I backed away and stuttered, "I . . . I. . . I . . . can . . . explain why we're out here."

Nereid burst out laughing, dropping to the ground in hysterics, and turning into our friend Bob. Bob was a Pond Punkie from the Proteusan (pro-tee-us-an) Clan whose power is shape shifting. Bob continued rolling around holding his chubby stomach while his long brown hair was tangled in some thorny plants.

"Really funny Bob," said Ace walking up to him and giving him a shove with his foot.

"You should've seen your faces," said Bob still laughing.

"You scared the bejeebers out of me," I said helping him up. "What are you doing out here?"

Bob caught his breath and said, "I was getting

one final look at the place before heading home to Proteus tomorrow. What are you two up to?"

Ace said, "We're going off grounds one last time." He didn't mention anything about his gel.

"Well, be careful. You better get out while the coast is clear," said Bob.

I felt along the prickly wall next to the gate for the secret opening Ace and I discovered on one of our trips out. We squeezed through the gap hidden by the vines. It was dark ahead of us as we made our way toward the Unknown Zone where the crevices were located that oozed Ace's gooey stuff. We never actually went into the Unknown Zone, only close enough to get the goo.

Ace's blue spikes glistened with frost from the frozen punkie gel. We slithered along on the cracks of the surface. I felt the webbing on my feet and hands warming up as the cracks released the inner heat of Neptune.

As we crept along the outskirts of the Unknown Zone, I heard a distant sound like someone talking.

Ace stopped crawling, looked at me, and asked, "Did you hear that?"

"Look, over there," I said pointing toward the Unknown Zone, just as Kroiser and Slate, two Pond Punkies from the Tritonan (Try-ton-an) Clan crawled under the elevated frozen gas ring into the Unknown Zone.

"Whoa, no one actually goes in the zone," said Ace. "Bad things happen in there."

"Word is, punkies go in and never come out," I added. "Maybe this is our chance to get rid of Kroiser for good."

"No way Blaze. The zone would spit him back out," said Ace laughing.

He did that a lot. Ace thought everything he did and said was funny. For the most part, everything he did and said was funny. That's why I liked hanging out with him.

I stood there wondering what attracted Kroiser to this creepy place.

Even though Kroiser was my age and the same

height as the rest of us, a whopping four inches, he seemed to tower over everyone with his evil ways. His scales reflected a different, more evil green than everyone else. Maybe that was from his trips in the Unknown Zone. I wondered how many times he went in there.

I stared over at the Zone. From the day we were born, we were told about the dangers of it. Amidst the frozen gases and swirly vapors, mysterious creatures existed. Even the Ancients, the most powerful Pond Punkies, feared the Unknown Zone.

"Let's get a little closer," I said, slowly creeping over to where Kroiser and Slate had slipped into the Zone.

I turned around and saw Ace still planted in the same place. He shook his head back and forth. He wouldn't come any closer.

My gills pulsated hard, but I inched nearer to the zone. It was creepy; the floating frozen gas ring surrounding it was thick and low tonight. I saw my reflection in it. Ace was right; my hair did look like fire. It was a little on the shaggy side. Down below my ears, but not quite covering my gills. My dad would have been pleased to see that. I had the toughest looking fiery red eyes, too.

"Not bad," I said to my reflection stumbling backwards. A horrible foul smell drifted out from the Unknown Zone stinging my nostrils and gills.

I had never smelled death, but other punkies said that's what it smelled like in the Unknown Zone. Now I knew what they meant.

I couldn't see Kroiser or Slate. I knew they went in right around here. I turned around again hoping to see Ace behind me, instead all I saw was the mist seeping out from the cracks and quickly freezing.

I inched a little closer reminding myself of the warnings from the Ancients. It was hard to hear myself think over the winds that howled. The wind gusted, pounding ice pellets against my scales. I crouched low, scuttling forward and crashed into a jagged ice column. I sure wished Ace was next to me.

I slowly poked my head under the gas ring peering into the darkness of the Unknown Zone. "Ahhhhh," I shrieked, jumping backwards. Two sets of webbed feet almost touched my nose. They had to belong to Kroiser and Slate. I didn't know if they heard me scream. I doubted it with how loud the wind howled. Then I wondered if they were still alive.

I stood up and the wind threw me against the frozen vapors. I dropped down to the smelly ground backing away from where I saw the feet. I stayed low moving a little bit further down. I closed my eyes tight, slid my head under the ring, and then opened my eyes.

The light was dim and the wind didn't howl. It was eerily quiet. Pointy ice columns were everywhere. I slowly crawled in. The ground was softer. My hands and knees left imprints in the surface as I crawled further into the Zone. My scales stiffened.

"Be brave Blazedale," my dad always said. I wondered if he would have said that now or maybe,

"What are you thinking? Get out of there!" If only he hadn't disappeared about a moon orbit ago. Gosh, I missed him so much.

Everything in me was saying, "Get out of here!" But I had to know why Kroiser had come in the Unknown Zone.

CHAPTER TWO

Tritonan's Secret

I hunkered down behind a smelly mound and suddenly the area on the other side of the mound glowed with a bright light.

Kroiser hissed, "Put that glow rock away. We don't want something in here to see us."

I poked my head around the side of the mound, lay still, and listened.

Kroiser stood there with his arms crossed over his chest, not scared of anything. He had a weird zigzag part in his white hair that looked like a crack

on Neptune's surface. Those icy white eyes seemed to match his evil inside. The scariest thing about him was a scar that started above his right eyebrow and stretched down his cheek. He refused to say how it got there, which was odd because Kroiser bragged about everything.

Slate's outstretched hand trembled with the glow rock resting in it. The light reflected off Slate's white hair casting a green glow on his abnormally large uneven ears. His white eyes grew larger as they locked on to his shaking hand. He slowly pulled his hand back slipping the glow rock into his pocket.

Kroiser said, "Slate, we need to be ready to enter the geyser when it erupts under the graduation ceremony tomorrow."

"Tomorrow, are you sure?" asked Slate.

"I can't believe Elder Triton has a nit-wit like you going on this mission," said Kroiser.

Kroiser had been my enemy at the academy since it became known that I was a twin and would go to Earth in the next geyser. He was just plain rotten to me, but then again he was pretty much rotten to everyone. Even so, he seemed especially jealous of me.

Twins were extremely rare and special to the Pond Punkie world. Only twins could telepathically communicate with each other. We could talk to each other in our minds no matter what the distance was between us.

A few moon orbits ago, a twin died on Neptune. That twin's sister was still on Earth. Those twins were the only form of communication with all the other Pond Punkies on Earth. When the twin on Neptune died, all contact with the Pond Punkies on Earth ended. Since his death, my sister, Ember, and I have received extra training in order to communicate between Earth and Neptune. That meant one of us would have to go to Earth. Before my dad disappeared, he had decided that it would be me.

Slate said, "I forgot Kroiser, what's the plan again?"

Kroiser let out a deep sigh and said, "How many times do I got to tell you? We go to Earth. We freeze the place and send the signal to Elder Triton who will then meet with the Secret Circle."

Slate shook his head and said, "Oh yeah. I remember now, but what signal? How you gonna do that?"

Kroiser seemed disgusted, throwing his hands in the air, and said, "Look, don't worry about the signal. I'll take care of that."

Slate snapped his fingers and said, "Oh yeah, I remember. That's when all the Tritonans get ready to blast to Earth."

A wicked grin came over Kroiser's face, and he said, "That's when we destroy this dark dump Neptune and all its moons. Then Earth will be our own planet like Triton was before it got sucked into Neptune's orbit."

"Oh my gosh," I groaned. Why would they want to destroy all the Pond Punkies and our home moons? My mom always said, "Blaze, keep a watchful eye when you are around a Tritonan." Did she know they were up to no good?

I gotta get out of here! I needed to warn the Elders. The Elders said the next scheduled geyser eruption was one moon orbit from now. And that was over by the small dark spot where all the geysers erupt. How could there be one tomorrow and no one knows about it? No geyser has ever erupted on the academy grounds.

Since all communication had been lost on Earth, there would be no way to warn the Pond Punkies to protect Earth from the Tritonan attack.

I started crawling backwards when Slate said, "Kroiser, do you think you will run into that twin's dad on Earth? You know the one that stopped you from entering the geyser a moon orbit ago and gave you that scar."

My dad? Alive on Earth! He must mean me. I'm the only twin.

Kroiser reached up running his finger the length of the jagged scar, smiled and said, "I hope so. This time I won't let him get away. Elder Triton has been secretly training me just for that encounter."

I knew my dad wasn't dead! Everyone else thought he was, but I knew he was alive! I needed to be in that geyser tomorrow and find him.

Suddenly my scales shivered. A small hairy creature, no bigger than one of my fingers, was crawling up Kroiser's webbed foot and then began to scuttle up his scaly leg. Kroiser swatted at the creature. His hand hit the thing, but the creature hung on. Kroiser didn't seem to notice it was still there.

Over their voices, I heard a sound like bones crunching. The ground vibrated. I caught a glimpse of "It" out of the corner of my right eye. The monster was massive, at least fifty times my size.

"Oh no!" I cried. Its green glowing eyes locked on to me.

CHAPTER THREE

Escape

I frantically tried to scoot back out of the zone. The ground violently shook as it charged at me! I sprung up, zigzagging around the ice columns, and sprinting back towards Ace.

"Run! Get out of here!" I shouted as I sped past him.

"I knew it. They're dead, aren't they? Something's after us, isn't it?" called Ace as he shot past me.

Up ahead a beam of light shot up to the stars from the center of the academy. Almost there!

We scaled the outer wall of the academy sprinting past the icy, grey Tritonan pod working our way toward the Naidan area.

Ace said, "What happened back there? What was after us?"

I said, "I don't know. All I know is it had six legs and gigantic teeth!"

I ran my hands over my scales and felt for any bumps.

"What are you doing?" asked Ace.

"Check my back side for me. Look for anything hairy and about the size of a finger."

I suddenly wondered about Kroiser and Slate. Had the creature gone back for them?

"I'm not touching you! Blaze, you better not have let anything out of there," Ace said. He backed away from me as if I had the cooties or something.

"I don't know if I took anything out of there unless you check my back." I pleaded.

Ace inched closer. "Turn around," he said. "But if something is on you, I'm not touching it, got it?"

"I got it," I said. I carefully studied my belly and arms. No creepy-crawly things that I could see.

"You're clean," said Ace as he slapped me on my back.

"Thanks, I owe you one," I said.

"Don't worry, I won't forget," said Ace with that stupid smile on his face.

"What was it like that close to the zone?" asked Ace.

"I wasn't close, I was in it! It smelled like death."

"That's what I heard," said Ace. "What were they doing in there?"

"That's what you're not going to believe. You know how some of the others are talking crazy about a geyser erupting under the graduation ceremony tomorrow?"

"Yeah," said Ace.

"Well Kroiser thinks it's really going to happen and so does Elder Triton," I said.

"I thought you weren't scheduled to go to Earth

for one more moon orbit," said Ace. He sat down behind a tall blue column by the entrance to the Naidan pod.

I paced back and forth and said, "I also learned my dad put that scar on Kroiser's face."

"What? I think being in that zone messed with your head. Your dad's been missing for at least a moon orbit now."

"Yeah, and that's about the same time Kroiser got that scar," I said. Then I told him everything I heard while I was in the Unknown Zone.

Ace's blue eyes got bigger and bigger. His mouth hung open replacing his usual grin.

"Well, say something," I said.

Ace closed his mouth, and then opened it again. He said, "Blaze, we need to be in that gey—"

I didn't hear the rest. Suddenly Nereid appeared next to Ace. I never knew when Nereid was around. He was from the Nereidan clan and had the power of invisibility.

If that's not Bob pretending to be Nereid, we're in trouble.

Nereid grabbed Ace by the back of his scaly neck with one hand, and grabbed me with the other.

"Nice try, Bob," said Ace reaching up to swat at Nereid's hand.

Nereid squeezed my shoulder harder and said, "So Bob has been shape shifting into me again."

Now I knew we were in trouble.

"Okay, you two may be able to spend another year here at the academy with me if you don't get in your pods immediately!" he shouted in our ears. As if we couldn't hear him right next to us.

"Nereid," I said as I tried to get out of his grip, but he only tightened it on my neck.

"No, don't even try to explain. I have had enough of you two sneaking around the academy for the last three moon orbits."

"But, I have to tell you something. It's important," I said.

"Yeah, real important, OUCH!" said Ace as Nereid squeezed him harder dragging us to our pods.

"It can wait until tomorrow," Nereid said and under his breath, I heard him say, "Hopefully after tomorrow I won't see you two ever again."

CHAPTER FOUR

Departure

I felt the excitement building in the air. Today was graduation day and maybe geyser eruption day. I wished my dad were here to see Ember and me graduating at the top of our clan. I missed him a ton. He would have known what to do about Kroiser. Nereid didn't even let me explain what happened.

I stood up looking around the crater. The crater was a big cavity smack in the middle of Neptune's

Training Academy. It was lined with our main source of light, glow rock. We held all our special celebrations here.

I wanted to locate Kroiser so I could keep an eye on him. "There you are," I thought, spotting him in the front row. He shouldn't be there. Only the top of each clan sat there and Kroiser was not at the top of the Tritonan Clan.

Just as I sat back down, I felt heat on the back of my neck and turned around to see none other than Finnegan. He put his webbed hands over his face. Finnegan was the only known Larissan to shoot flames out of his gills instead of his hands like the rest of us Larissans.

Finnegan looked down at his webbed feet and said, "Sorry Blaze, really I'm sorry. I wasn't trying to torch you."

I watched him silently. Finnegan stared at the ground moving his feet in a circle on the ice.

"I thought you weren't graduating if you couldn't

laugh without shooting flames out of your gills?"

"I did stop. Now they only come out of my nose every now and then."

I laughed at this and so did Finnegan.

WHOOSH! Flames shot out of his nostrils, just missing my back, and creating a puddle of water on the surface by our feet.

Finnegan slumped back in his seat clamping his webbed hands over his nose and said, "I'm a little nervous, Blaze. The Academy already held me back one orbit. It wouldn't look good to have a Pond Punkie on the four orbit plan."

I said, "Its okay Finnegan. Listen, I may need your help today."

Finnegan raised his webbed hand, saluted me, and said, "At your service Blaze. What do you need me to do?"

I told Finnegan what happened last night and then said, "So watch my back and also keep an eye on Kroiser."

I turned to face Ember, my twin sister, sitting to

the left of me. Her hair was the same flame color as mine, but a lot neater. Ember wore it long and straight. She never had a hair out of place. She looked more like our mom sitting there with her back straight.

Ember was punkie prim and proper.

I was on the sloppy side.

She was all scientific and sure about everything.

For twins we were pretty much opposite.

She had a hand in her pocket. All of us Pond Punkies have two built in pockets above our hips.

"What do you have in your pocket Em?"

Ember said, "Well, Blazedale."

She refused to call me Blaze. I told her several times Blazedale was not cool.

Ember went on, "Actually, it is the most interesting thing. I found it yesterday over by the scooter. You know the place, Blazedale, between the Great Dark Spot and the Small Dark Spot."

"You shouldn't be over there Em. It's not safe."

"Don't worry, I was careful. Krystal went with me."

"Ember, remember what mom said about the Tritonans?"

Ember said, "Krystal is different. She is not like the rest of the Tritonans. Besides, she doesn't make fun of my pocket pals."

Ember always picked up small dead frozen creatures she found on Neptune. She carried them in small pouches in her pockets. The other Pond Punkies teased Em about this strange habit. They called what she carried around in her pockets, pocket pals.

Ember didn't care. She analyzed her pocket pals and wondered what they were like when they were alive.

After our dad disappeared, she secretly told me she wished she were the twin Dad chose to send to Earth. She wanted to study the live creatures on Earth.

Pond Punkies scuttled about everywhere in the crater. It looked like a rainbow on the move. White, green, black, silver, red, blue, brown, and yellow haired Pond Punkies tried to locate their seats before the ceremony began.

I looked out at the skies and saw my home moon Larissa shining bright over the ceremony.

"Look at that," said Ember in amazement. She giggled, pointing to our right.

A couple of rows down, Ace sprung out of his seat. His aqua blue hair stood straight up—like it was standing at attention.

"How did he make his hair do that?" Ember asked.

"He created punkie gel."

"Punkie gel?"

"Yeah, it's his big secret for graduation day. Let's you do anything you want with your hair. He's hoping all the other punkies will want some before going home. He thinks he's going to get rich."

Ace headed our way. "Looking good," he said to Ember.

He turned to face me and said, "Hey Blaze, we need to talk."

Ember said, "Caulder," she used Ace's real name. "I like your hair."

Ace pointed a webbed finger at her, made a couple of clicking sounds with his mouth and with a wink of his eye said, "Right back atcha."

Ember giggled and said, "I might just have to order some of that gel."

I nudged Ace's arm pointing at Nereid with his long pointed nose, little beady, silver eyes, and his ratty short silver hair. He walked to the middle of the crater and started to climb to the top of a magnificent block of ice.

I said, "The ceremony is about to start."

Ace leaned in and whispered in my ear, "I gotta tell ya. I'm not ready to go to Earth, but if that geyser goes off today, I'm there for you. I'll hold them back. You get in that geyser, find your dad, and stop the Tritonans."

Ace didn't wait for a reply. He turned and ran to get to his seat.

"Excellent," I thought. Now I got Finnegan and Ace to watch my back. Then it was there, the question that kept me up last night, "Can I do this?"

I heard a voice in my head and realized Ember was listening to my thoughts.

She said, "Blazedale, what was Ace talking about? What is this stuff about going to Earth? Who are you stopping? And Dad's there?" Ember frowned.

I telepathically told her everything that happened last night at the Unknown Zone while Nereid went on with his boring speech.

Ember's sparkling red eyes were as round as her open mouth. The green color of her face turned pale yellow. Suddenly, a low moaning sound came from under my feet. The frozen ground trembled moving my feet with it. Ember clasped her shaking hand around my wrist and asked, "What's happening, Blazedale?"

Our seats shattered and the sound roared like a super nova explosion.

I squeezed her hand tight shouting, "HANG ON! GEYSER!"

A pillar of blue steam erupted in the center of the crater underneath the ice sculpture blasting it into space. Glow rock hurled past us. I held on tight to Ember's hand falling to the ground.

I needed to get Ember out of here and get in that geyser. I had to find Ace.

Punkies screamed running away from the geyser. Debris littered the crater as Neptune continued gushing out her insides. I felt Ember's fear in my mind. "Ember you have to get out of here!"

Ember's voice said weakly in my head, "Blazedale, you are going to do great things." She let go of my hand crawling toward safety.

I heard Krystal yell, "Ember, this way!"

Kroiser and Slate dodged the raining glow rocks making their way toward the geyser.

"Noooooo!" I shouted staggering along the erupting ground. I had to get between Kroiser and the geyser.

"Wait for me!" shouted Finnegan, running to catch up.

Five more Tritonans joined Kroiser and Slate marching towards the geyser.

Ace shot out of nowhere lodging his scaly body at the edge of the geyser blocking the Tritonans path. He raised his webbed hands aiming them at the blue liquid spewing out of the geyser and used his Naiadan power. A huge blue hand sprung out striking the Tritonans.

Kroiser hurled to the ground along with two of his buddies.

I shouted, "Way to go Ace!" running to his side with Finnegan next to me.

Ace created a whirlpool aiming it at the remaining Tritonans. Kroiser sprang to his feet.

The Tritonans raised their arms opening their palms turning Ace's whirlpool to ice. It crashed to the ground in a million frozen pieces.

I steadied my body next to Ace shouting over the roar, "That's your plan?"

Ace gave me that crazy grin and Finnegan shouted, "Jump in Blaze! We'll hold them."

I turned to jump and Kroiser clung on my back.

He yelled in my ear, "Not without me!"

Together we slammed into the geyser.

I heard in my head Ember's desperate scream, "BLAZEDALE, HELP MEeeee!"

CHAPTER FIVE

The Arrival

I felt a sharp pain on the side of my face.

SMACK! There it was again. I slowly opened my eyes just in time to jerk my head away from the next slap.

"STOP! I'M AWAKE!" I shouted. My body felt warm, light, almost weightless, but my head ached.

"You're alive! Excellent!" cried Ace.

My eyes focused on an entire new world. Everything was bright and green. "Are those trees?"

I asked. "WOW! This water it's so warm." I paddled around barely feeling my battle wounds. Trees surrounded the pond looking like the drawings we had at NTA.

"Ace, what are you doing here? Kroiser jumped in the geyser with me, not you."

"I saw Kroiser tackle you and I jumped in too. What are friends for?"

I had to think back to geyser travel class. The Elders said after entering the Earth's atmosphere we usually landed in the pond on the Whitney Estate.

"Ace, we need to figure out where we are and find shelter. Remember from training, daylight is only so long here. Did you see Kroiser anywhere?"

"I didn't look for Kroiser. I thought you were dead."

I swam around with Ace by my side looking for Kroiser and the other Tritonans. I kept an eye out for any indication that we were in the Whitney Pond.

"Look over there. Floating on the surface," I said pointing off in the distance. I started to swim close to a Pond Punkie floating in the water.

"Blaze, wait! It could be a trick. We need a plan."

I said, "Yeah like your plan back at the graduation ceremony?"

"Okay, I'll give you that one, but I'm here," said Ace slapping me gently upside my head.

"Come on Ace follow me." I went under water and swam a little deeper heading toward the floating punkie.

Red hair drifted in the water. My gills fluttered. Please don't be Ember.

We raced up to Finnegan floating lifeless in the water. He jumped in the geyser too! I grabbed one arm and Ace grabbed the other. We stood him up in the water. I wrapped my arms around his chest and Ace let go.

"Ace, slap him like you did me."

"No way," said Ace. He swam back a little. "He's dead Blaze. Look at him."

Finnegan's head hung lifeless. His chin touched his chest and water droplets rolled off of his curly hair.

My hands trembled as I held Finnegan tighter. "Please be okay Finny," I cried.

I shouted at Ace, "JUST DO IT ACE! SLAP HIM!"

Ace swam forward quickly slapping Finnegan. Nothing happened.

"Do it again," I said.

Ace shook his head no. We were both crying now.

"Please Ace, try once more."

Ace reached up slapping Finnegan again.

I felt Finny's body jerk.

"He's alive!" I shouted.

Finny opened his eyes with water spilling out of his nose and mouth.

I asked, "You okay Finny?"

"I...don't...know...yet. I guess I am," he said in a raspy voice.

I held on to Finnegan with one arm turning him around with my other arm so he faced me.

"Wow," said Finnegan, looking over my shoulder. "This place is amazing. Everything looks so alive and green. It all matches the drawings from the academy.

"Are you okay to swim?" I asked Finnegan.

He pulled away from my grip kicking his webbed feet. He propelled forward, changed direction and swam back to face me.

"This water is awesome. Why is it so warm?" asked Finnegan.

"Look up," I said pointing to the sun. "Finny, did you see Ember anywhere before you jumped in the geyser?"

He hesitated and said, "No Blaze. All I saw was you, Kroiser, Ace and the other Tritonans jump in.

I figured you would need my services, so I leaped in too. What happened to Kroiser and his friends?"

Ace said, "We don't know. He isn't here."

I spun around scanning the shoreline. "Oh great. There it is!" I shouted.

"What is it? Is it them?" asked Ace.

"No, it's that," I said pointing to a circular building behind a row of tall trees. The building had a huge dome on top of it with a cylinder aiming at the sky.

Finnegan said, "That building must be the Whitney Observatory they told us about at NTA."

Ace did a somersault in the water and said, "Alright, old man Whitney can help us."

I said, "The Elders did say he was our contact on Earth and that the Whitney Estate was a safe place."

"THERE YOU ARE!" a voice cried out from the shore.

CHAPTER SIX

Trapped

SPLASH! SPLASH! Something charged in the water toward us. It was massive, white and had a bubble for a head.

Ace cried out, "What is that?"

I shouted, "Quick, underwater!"

GOOSH! A net scooped up the three of us.

WOOSH! I shot a flame at the bubble seeing the human's face. I tumbled out of the net on top of Ace and Finny crashing to the bottom of something hard and cold.

SLAM! Suddenly it was dark.

We lurched to the left, crashed to the right, ending up in a pile.

"Sorry," squeaked Finnegan from the bottom.

"Eeww, what's that smell?" asked Ace quickly rolling off Finny.

Finnegan farted a nasty one.

"I gotta get out of here," said Ace.

BAM! We slammed down.

CREEK. Light streamed in. Ace got into position. Finny and I stood at the ready aiming our hands at the opening.

"AHHHH!" All three of us screamed as a gigantic white hand snatched us out plopping us on a counter covered with shiny gadgets that lit up and crackled with static. Beeps sounded from all directions.

The three of us huddled our backs together in a circle. We were ready to attack from all sides when the human spoke.

I said, "Can't understand you with that bubble on your head."

The human pressed three buttons on the neck of his outfit removing the bubble.

A young human boy with glasses crooked on his face and short blond hair sticking out everywhere said, "I am William R. Whitney IV, the great grandson of William R. Whitney and this is no bubble. This is an Apollo 17 Helmet. It is an exact replica of the authentic NASA Apollo 17 Space Suit. Good thing I had it on or you would have burned me."

Finnegan leaned over by my ear and said, "He said is name is Whitney. Can we trust him?"

"I think so," I said.

Ace said, "I don't trust anyone who throws me in a dark cell."

"I'm sorry about that," said William. "I didn't know how else to get you in the observatory. My Great Grandfather said I needed to be at the pond and get an important message to the fire twin." He opened a blue book on the counter by our feet. "This is GG's journal. GG is what I call my Great Grandfather."

Ace and Finnegan stared at the pages in the journal. "Wow," I said looking at drawings of Pond Punkies from different clans using their powers.

I said, "My name is Blaze, that's Ace with the blue spikes and Finnegan with the curly red hair. They told us at our training academy to contact your Great Grandfather when we arrive on Earth. Is he around?"

William's eyes started to tear up. He wiped at them and said, "I can't take you to see GG because he died two weeks ago."

"Whoa," said Ace.

"I'm sorry, William," I said. "You must really miss him."

William nodded his head blowing his nose.

WOOF! WOOF! The noise sounded like it was coming up from a tunnel. A hairy beast shot out from an opening across the room. A large tongue hung out of its mouth flapping in the air while its tail swung madly back and forth. It looked like it belonged in the Unknown Zone. Its eyes locked on me. I shot a pillar of fire at it. William jumped in between the raging monster and my flame.

William shouted, "WAIT! Don't hurt him. He's GG's dog, Butler." He bent down talking to the beast, "Good boy, Butler. Don't worry. They're friends."

Butler plopped his paws on the counter. He put his wet black nose on my face, licked, and lifted my body off the ground.

"Eeww, that's gross," said Ace.

"I might want to give it a try," said Finny, laughing for the first time since arriving on Earth. Flames shot out of his nose, Butler yelped and backed away. All of us laughed at this.

I wiped Butler's drool off me asking William, "When was the last time Butler saw a Pond Punkie?"

William flipped through some pages in the journal and said, "Here it is. GG wrote this about a year ago." William read aloud, "*A Larissan Pond Punkie arrived in the pond today. He's different from the others. Not at all excited about being on Earth. He said he wasn't supposed to be here. He needed to get back home to Larissa. He mentioned fire twins and revealed a prophecy. He said his name was Brogan.*"

"I knew it!" I shouted. "My dad is alive!" I started pacing. Warmth flooded through my body and my heartbeat raced. I quickly brushed away the tear gathering in my eye.

"Your dad?" asked William. "Are you and Finnegan the fire twins?"

Ace burst out laughing.

"No," I said. "Hopefully my sister is still on Neptune."

William flipped pages back to the beginning of the book and said, "You may want to take a look at this."

The words were close to what we learned in Earth Language Class. The date of the journal entry was seventy-two moon orbits ago. It mentioned the first time GG found a Pond Punkie. Her name was Arianna, the first Pond Punkie twin to land on Earth. GG helped her and they became friends. GG vowed to protect the pond on the Whitney Estate and the Pond Punkies vowed to protect Earth.

William closed the book and said, "GG told me before he died that Arianna is always close by. I haven't seen her and GG said she would help me find you."

I hoped nothing happened to Arianna and my dad.

CHAPTER SEVEN

Prophecy

"William, what about that Prophecy you mentioned earlier?" I asked.

William said, "It's here in the journal." He pushed buttons on a board laying the book on a shiny surface. The screen in front of us came to life with letters bigger than I have ever seen before.

Across the top of the page it had written *MUST DECODE* and below that *PROPHECY*.

I began to read aloud.

The fire twins will land
 The chosen one manned
With a mission for all
A fire ring in hand

Clear it will become soon
On the eve of the blue moon
Sound waves warn the clans
A danger to Earth and Neptune

Trust the temperature will be chilled
As the mission is fulfilled
But pay attention you must
Or many may be killed

Consider this a tattle
Whether in L.A., New York, Miami,
 or Seattle
Pond Punkie clans will arrive
One will do battle

Count on one more
To help even the score
To protect the fire twin's back
As the battle soars

Take time to look behind
You will be certain to find
All must arrive back home
For the sake of mankind

I said, "That's some of the worst poetry I ever read."

"GG said it wasn't poetry it was a Prophecy and needed to be decoded," said William.

Ace leaned over and whispered in my ear, "You're a twin and you're the only one I know of who can do that fire ring thing."

I said, "Yeah, but not from my hands. I'm worried about Ember. I still don't feel her in my mind and this Prophecy said the fire twins will land. It said twins, plural, more than one. Was she in the geyser too?"

Above my head, a large black cylinder poked out of the ceiling moving in circles.

I said, "Uh . . . why is that thing moving up there?"

"That's not possible," said William. "You would need to push this button on the keyboard to make the telescope move."

POOF! The most beautiful Nereidan Pond Punkie I ever saw appeared by the keyboard. Her silver hair shimmered flowing down past her shoulders. Her eyes looked like liquid mercury. She looked about as old as Nereid.

"Blaze, allow me to introduce myself. My name is Arianna." She bowed down before me. No one had ever bowed down to me before, so I bowed back. She looked like a queen.

I asked, "How did you know I'm Blaze?"

She flashed a brilliant smile and said, "I have been listening in on your conversation."

"Ahemmmm," William made a noise and said,

Excuse me." He leaned in closer to Arianna. "I am William R. Whitney the Fourth."

Arianna turned, bowing to William. He bowed to her. Arianna said, "William R. Whitney IV, I am much honored to meet you and sorry for the loss of your Great Grandfather. He was a dear friend of mine over the last seventy-two moon orbits or years if you prefer. He has always spoken highly of you. Even though you are only eleven years of age, your Great Grandfather entrusted you with a mission beyond your years."

William asked, "Where have you been?"

She said, "When GG passed away, I went to tell the Pond Punkies on Earth of our great loss. GG realized because of the way the stars were aligning the prophecy was going to happen soon. GG used all of his devices in the observatory and could predict when a geyser would erupt on Neptune. He always showed up at the pond to greet the new arrivals."

Arianna touched my shoulder, "He also knew that a Larissan twin was scheduled to come to Earth in the next geyser. That is how he knew the prophecy referred to the eve of this blue moon."

I asked Arianna, "Do you know where my dad is?"

"I looked for him throughout the tunnel system, but couldn't find him. Blaze, we need to decipher this prophecy. GG was correct with the fire twin landing and the date. He passed away before we had a chance to talk about everything in the Prophecy. He told me to get the prophecy to you."

HOWLLLLL, HOWLLLLL, Butler howled. A screeching sound rushed through my head pounding my ears. It was higher pitched than Butler's howling. The color drained from Arianna's beautiful face. Ace and Finnegan buckled over with their webbed hands covering their ears.

CHAPTER EIGHT

The Signal

"What's that noise?" I shouted.

William said, "What noise? Stop that, Butler. You're hurting their ears."

The noise stopped as quickly as it started. Butler stopped howling.

"Arianna, are you okay?" I asked.

Arianna said, "That noise was the Tritonans using their crystal sound waves as a beacon."

I said, "Crystal what?"

Arianna said, "I heard in the tunnels about the

Tritonans holding a secret meeting. All the Tritonans on earth will head toward that one crystal sound wave. Evidently, our friend Butler can hear this sound wave, too."

"Arianna, William, I have to tell you what happened on Neptune the night before the geyser erupted." I told them everything. I included how Nereid didn't let me explain.

BEEP, BEEP, BEEP. . . All of us turned toward the beeping sound. It came from William.

Arianna said, "William, I believe you are beeping."

"Oh yeah, this is my world news alert. A new gadget that alerts me to all the breaking news."

William looked down at a small silver box attached to his space suit. He smiled.

"I know where the Tritonans are," he said.

"How could you know that?" I tried to see what was on the screen of the gadget.

"Because Lakes are frozen in Florida," said William.

"So? When you're from Neptune, frozen things are hardly unusual," I said.

"It's 92 degrees in Florida!" said William.

"That's impossible," said Finnigan.

"That could mean only one thing..." Ace said, not finishing his thoughts.

William pressed some buttons on the keyboard. A screen full of people replaced the words of the Prophecy.

I listened to a head talking on the screen. It said ponds and lakes in central Florida froze over without any explanation. Then they showed a little boy standing by a frozen pond in Lake Mary. He held a frozen animal.

The little boy said, "This is Luther my cat." The boy started to cry and said, "I . . . I don't know how Luther got like this."

Arianna said, "We have no time to spare. You three, come with me." She bolted to a bookshelf.

"Wait!" shouted William. He pulled open a drawer taking something out. "GG mentioned these in his journal. I don't know if they work. You put one of these in your ear and press this button." He used the tip of a pencil to show where the button was located. "They have a built in microphone.

You will be able to hear and speak to each other or to me."

Ace ran up to William's hand grabbing one. The rest of us did the same. I didn't want to put something strange in my ear, but I was excited about the chance to use one of GG's gadgets.

William pressed some more buttons on what looked like a control panel and turned some knobs. He leaned his mouth up to an object on a stick and said, "Test 1, 2, 3."

"Ahhhhh!" we all shouted.

"Sorry," said William turning a knob and speaking again, "Test 1, 2, 3."

I heard him just fine. His voice in my head reminded me of how Ember and I talked to each other. I hoped Ember was safe and still on Neptune.

"Can everyone hear me?" he asked.

We all said, "Yes." I heard our voices coming out of a box behind me.

"Okay, now we can talk to each other," said William.

Arianna tugged at a book, pulled it back and jumped into the opening.

I heard her in my ear saying, "Quickly, jump in."

Ace pushed me out of the way and leaped in. "Ahhhhhhh," was all I heard.

I gestured with my hand for Finnegan to go next.

I flew in after him. My body slid fast, twisting, and turning in all directions. "Ahhhhhhhhhhhhh!" I yelled picking up speed and then SPLASH! The water felt warm and was clear enough to see the others ahead of me.

Arianna stopped in front of some green fuzzy plants.

"There." Arianna pointed to a hole in the bottom of the pond.

"What's that?" asked Finnegan.

"It's part of a network of major and minor tunnels that we use to travel throughout the Earth.

Arianna paused, and then said softly, "We lost all contact with Neptune when my twin Alexander died."

Arianna turned to Ace and said, "Ace you

will wait here in case anyone shows up early for tomorrow's full moon meeting. Every full moon, Pond Punkies from all over the world come here to see if there has been any contact with Neptune."

Ace looked around and asked, "By myself?"

I said, "You'll be okay Ace. You can talk to us through the ear thingy."

Finnegan swam up to Arianna, saluted her and said, "Finnegan here, at your service."

She said, "Finnegan and Blazedale, you two come with me."

Arianna swam to the tunnel opening. Finnegan and I followed. The fuzzy plant tickled my scales and I turned around to make sure Finnegan didn't laugh.

SWOOSH! The tunnel sucked in Arianna.

Finnegan's eyes grew larger and he said, "You first."

I stuck my foot in the opening feeling an unseen force yanking my body in the tunnel. SWOOSH! "Ahhhh!" I moved at lightening speed.

"Ahhhh!" I heard in my ear. Finnegan entered the tunnel.

"What's happening? Are you okay?" said Ace. "Talk to me."

I flew towards a fork in the tunnel thinking I was going to hit the side of the wall when I heard Arianna say, "Lean to your left at the fork in the tunnel."

I leaned and another tunnel sucked me in. The tunnels glowed dimly. Arianna shimmered in front of me. I was too scared to turn around and check on Finnegan.

Arianna said, "Leave the tunnel system on the next opening to your right."

There it was. I swerved to my right aiming for the opening.

CHAPTER NINE

Luther

BAM! I slammed into Arianna and Finnegan smashed into me.

We sat on the bottom of a lake in an opening just big enough for the three of us.

"What happened?" I asked, helping Arianna up."

"We hit ice," she said. "You two will need to thaw this lake with your powers."

"Hold on. I need to catch my breath. That tunnel travel was amazing." I said.

"No doubt," said Finnegan.

I heard in my earpiece, "You're so lucky." It was Ace. "I wish I was with you guys."

I said, "Arianna, I don't know. Usually it's a whole bunch of us Larissans that thaw the ice to practice our water sports. It was never just two of us."

"We can do it, Blaze," said Finnegan.

"Okay Finny, let's give it a try," I said.

We all backed up as far as possible without entering the tunnel. Finnegan and I turned to face the ice. "AHHHH!" I shouted. An enormous open mouth with two rows of sharp jagged teeth stared at us.

I asked, "What is that thing?"

Arianna said, "Don't worry about that, it is just a fish. They are in the water all over Earth. Just be sure to keep your distance from them or you may end up as its next meal."

I stared at this creature, not wanting to be its late night snack.

Arianna said, "Blaze and Finnegan, you must do it now. Remember from your training at the academy. Once a Tritonan freezes something, a Larissan only has a short time to thaw it in order for it to survive.

Finnegan and I held up both our hands, aimed our open palms toward the frozen water, looked at each other, and shouted together, "To the Power of Neptune!" WHOOSH! WHOOSH! Flames shot out of my palms, but only a spark came out of Finnegan's palms.

"Come on, Finny. You can do it!" I shouted to him.

I held my flames aimed at the ice and saw Finnegan closing his eyes. He mumbled something. Then WHOOSH! Flames shot out of his palms.

"I'm doing it! I'm doing it!" he shouted.

"Way to go, Finny," said Ace in the ear gadget.

Water gushed over us. The thawed fish turned and rapidly swam away. We didn't stop until there was no more ice

I shouted, "Awesome! We did it."

"Well done you two," Arianna said.

"Excellent," said William in my ear.

Arianna said, "Be careful. We don't want any humans to see us. As a Nereidan, I can share my power of invisibility as long as we are touching."

Finnegan quickly touched Arianna and vanished. I held her hand and disappeared. We surfaced to the sun glistening on the pond. People pointed, gawking at the thawed lake.

Finnegan said, "There, to our right. The little boy!"

Arianna said, "Finnegan, please wait here, just under the water."

I let go of Arianna's hand, turned to face her and confessed. "Back at the academy, I set a Pond Punkie on fire when I tried thawing him. What if I burn his cat?"

She squeezed my hand to make us invisible and said, "Blaze, you won't burn the cat. You will do just fine."

We swam to the shore together. From there, we walked out of the lake by trees shaped differently than the trees at the Whitney Estate. Each branch was long, green, and wavy. It looked like someone attached brown balls at the top of it. We stopped in front of the boy holding his cat.

The cat's hair was all black except for around its nose and the end of its four legs where it was white.

The boy cradled Luther, as a mother would hold a baby punkie. Luther's frozen legs stuck straight up in the air. People gathered around the boy.

I hoped Arianna couldn't feel my hand trembling. I aimed both of my hands at the cat to thaw it and became visible.

"Uh-oh," I said. The little boy looked down right at me. Arianna touched my back making me invisible again.

Arianna whispered, "Now, Blaze, do it now."

I aimed my hands and my invisible flames hit Luther. I kept them aimed on him until Luther's feet started jerking. Ice cracked off them. His long black tail swished back and forth. Ice melted and dripped from him.

MEOWWW! MEOWWW! "Luther, you're alive, you're alive!" shouted the little boy hugging his cat.

Arianna said, "Now let us get back to the pond. Quick!"

She pulled my hand running towards the pond.

We paused at the edge of the water and that's when I saw him.

"Look!" I said. "Over there between those two trees. Do you see him? It's a Tritonan. Let's go get him." I let go of Arianna, turned to run toward the Tritonan, and became visible again.

I had to stop that. I touched Arianna again. It was too late. The Pond Punkie disappeared.

Finnegan came through my ear gadget, "I saw him, Blaze. It was a Tritonan, but it didn't look like Kroiser."

Arianna and I dove into the lake. We all headed for the bottom. The murky water made it difficult to see the tunnel. Arianna stayed close to Finnegan and me. We stopped right outside the tunnel opening.

"I'm sorry, Arianna. I think that Tritonan saw us because of my stupidity."

Arianna said, "You just thawed this lake. I am sure that is what he noticed. Remember you are no longer a punkie in training at the academy."

"I'm also not the chosen one," I said.

Arianna said, "We will discuss that back at the observatory."

At the tunnel opening Arianna said, "This time we will go north then west. Follow me like before."

SWOOOSH! Again, the tunnel system sucked us in.

CHAPTER TEN

The Chosen One

"Owww . . . Nooooo," I heard Arianna pleading in my ear.

"What's happening?" said William. "Is someone hurt?"

"Blaze, are you okay?" asked Finnegan.

I said, "I think something happened to Arianna. I can't see her."

Ace said, "Arianna, are you okay?" She didn't answer.

We exited the tunnel at the Whitney Pond.

Slowly, she became visible. She lay on the bottom of the lake outside the opening to the tunnel. Beautiful Arianna had shiny ice slivers sticking out of her everywhere.

I held her and asked, "What happened?" I gently removed a few slivers. Arianna groaned with each one plucked from her scales.

She said weakly, "Be careful, Blaze, they are deadly. A Tritonan with ice slivers attacked me in the tunnels. I believe they wanted to stop you."

I said, "What are ice slivers?"

Arianna whispered, "Only the best of the best have this ability. It is very rare. Before my brother died, the Elders said a young Tritonan at the academy had this rare power. He would be about your age."

"Kroiser," Ace and I said at the same time. He must have survived the trip to Earth.

Arianna's eyes started to close. She spoke in barely a whisper, "Remember Blaze, you . . . are. . .

the . . . chosen . . . one. Work with Wil . . ." Her voice faded.

I cried, "No! You'll be okay."

Finnegan and I leaned closer to her lips and heard her say," Count on one more to . . ." She disappeared. Ice slivers floated to the surface.

I said, "What just happened? Where is Arianna?" I looked around for her to reappear.

This was my fault. I let that Tritonan see me.

"What's going on down there?" came through my ear. It was William.

"She's dead," said Finnegan.

William said, "I'll meet you on the shore."

I watched as Ace and Finnegan swam to the surface.

I turned and entered the tunnel. SWOOSH! The tunnel swallowed me. I didn't care where it took me as long as it took me away from the Whitney Estate and that dumb prophecy. Sorry Arianna, you have the wrong chosen one.

BAM! SLAM! "Owwww, what did I hit?" PHEW! I flew out a tunnel opening into a lake and I wasn't alone.

Nereid looked surprised to see me.

He stood up and said, "Are you okay, Blazedale?"

I didn't get up; I sat on the bottom of the lake looking at him and answered, "Yeah, unfortunately I'm okay. I thought you were dead, blasted into space with the ice sculpture."

"Luckily, I survived," said Nereid. "These tunnels take some getting used to." He reached a hand out to help me up.

"Don't touch me!" I yelled. "You wouldn't listen to me. I tried to warn you about the geyser. Now I don't know if Ember is safe on Neptune, I can't find my dad and Kroiser killed Arianna."

Nereid's face paled with this news. He backed up and said, "Blazedale, I was wrong. I should have listened to you and Caulder. I'm on my way to the

Whitney Estate. I heard in the tunnels about the full moon meeting tomorrow. What happened to Arianna?"

"You'll find out at the meeting. You didn't happen to see my dad, did you?" I asked.

"No, but everyone keeps talking about the arrival of a fire twin needed to fulfill a Prophecy." said Nereid. He raised an eyebrow when he said fire twin.

"I have to go." I turned toward the tunnel. Nereid grabbed my arm pulling me back.

"Blazedale, they say the fire twin is the chosen one."

"Well it's not me," I said. "Got to go. I'm looking for my dad." SWOOSH! The tunnel sucked me in. A picture of Arianna covered in ice slivers flashed in my mind and what she said. "Remember Blaze, you are the chosen one."

I quickly turned around and headed back to Nereid, shooting out of the opening. Nereid stood there with his arms crossed over his chest. I thought I saw the start of a smile.

"Nereid," I said. "I need to tell you what happened that night you caught Ace and me sneaking out?"

"Which night?" asked Nereid, now fully smiling.

"The night before graduation," I said.

I told him everything about that night and then about Arianna being attacked with ice slivers. I slumped down on the bottom of the lake putting my hands over my face.

Nereid reached down pulling my hands apart so I had to look at him and said, "Blazedale, the Elders heard of some secret meeting the Tritonans were holding."

I asked Nereid, "Why would the Tritonans want to destroy all the other Pond Punkie Clans and our home moons?"

Nereid sat next to me putting his arm around my shoulder. I stiffened my back. He said, "Listen. Blazedale, many, many moon orbits ago, Triton was its own planet. Neptune's gravity was so powerful it sucked Triton into its orbit beginning a bad relationship. The Tritonans do not want to orbit a planet. They want to be a planet. Some say that is why it circles opposite of all the other moons in constant opposition. The Elders thought we were at peace with the Tritonan Pond Punkies.

I heard the crystal sound wave earlier signaling Tritonan war. We need to get to the Whitney Observatory and start planning our attack."

"I'm not going back, Nereid. I'm going to look for my dad."

"Blazedale, only you can make that decision." Nereid stood up swimming to the tunnel opening.

"Wait!" I shouted standing up and swimming to him. I blew. PHOOF! A fire ring shot out of my mouth. It floated up toward the surface until I shot a fire arrow at it from my hands. The arrow hit the fire ring causing it to disappear.

Nereid's face seemed to glow showing signs of a smile.

"I know," I said. "Now I know how Finnegan feels. That prophecy states the chosen one will be manned with a mission for all, a fire ring in his hand. I can't make a fire ring come out of my hand. I'm a chosen reject."

Nereid smiled and began laughing a deep gut-wrenching laugh.

I said, "Great you think I'm a joke too." I started to enter the tunnel when Nereid pulled me back.

"Blazedale, see that thing swimming over there?"

"It's only a fish," I said. "Arianna said to stay away from them."

"Come with me," said Nereid, pulling me with him as he swam toward the fish. At least he pulled me by my arm and not my neck like he did all the time at the academy.

He said, "Put an imprisonment ring around that fish."

"A what?" I asked. "What are you talking about?"

Nereid said, "Your fire rings are called

imprisonment rings. You blow them out of your mouth controlling them with your hands. They hold someone or something until breaking the ring with your arrow. Only you can break the rings. They cannot be extinguished with water or freezing over."

"Wow," was all I could say. I felt better now that I knew the fire rings were supposed to come out of my mouth.

I puckered up my mouth shaping it in a circle, and blew. PHOOF! A fire ring shot out floating to the surface.

Nereid came up behind me. He grabbed my arm, raised it facing my open palm at the fire ring, and told me to say, "To the Power of Neptune."

"To the Power of Neptune," I shouted at the floating ring. It stopped where it was. Nereid held on to my arms moving them in the direction of the fish.

"Wow!" I said. The fire ring moved toward the fish.

Nereid let go of my arms.

"What happened?" I asked. "The ring moved by using my arms, then just stopped."

"You broke your concentration, Blazedale, breaking your control. You must focus on your goal, imprisoning your target."

"I'll try again," I said. I found another fish, puckering up, I blew. PHOOF! Another fire ring shot out and started floating away. I raised my arms opening my palms and said, "To the Power of Neptune." I moved my outstretched palm toward the fish. I concentrated moving the fire ring closer, closer.

"Now, quickly!" said Nereid.

I encircled the fish. The fish looked like a statue in a fire ring floating in place.

"Yeah, I did it!" I shouted. "But will that hurt it?"

"No, it won't remember a thing."

We swam to the imprisoned fish. Reaching up, I poked it with my finger. It didn't move.

Nereid poked his finger at the fish, causing him to fly backwards.

"What happened?" I asked.

Nereid said, "It's your force field protecting what you imprisoned. Only you can enter it. No one can release it or hurt it. Now shoot the flaming arrow and release the fish."

I backed up some not wanting to be too close when it was free again. I raised my arm, opened my hand, aiming my palm at the fish. A fire arrow shot out of my hand traveling straight through the water. It hit the fire ring freeing the fish.

I said, "Ace is going to go nuts when he sees this."

Nereid said, "Blazedale, you will need to have complete control of these imprisonment rings to use them on the Tritonans."

"I don't know Nereid. That was only a fish and he couldn't kill me with ice slivers. I'm not so sure about using these on Tritonans."

"Blazedale, we need to get to the Whitney observatory and figure out what the Tritonans are doing. You can practice your imprisonment rings there."

I said, "What if that prophecy meant Ember? Maybe she can blow fire rings too. I never told her I could. I don't have a good feeling about this chosen one stuff."

Nereid said, "We should stay together, Blazedale. It would be safer."

I thought about Arianna covered in the ice slivers and said, "Okay, I'll go with you."

Nereid and I entered the tunnel entrance. SWOOSH! I liked how that felt when the tunnel pulled me in.

CHAPTER ELEVEN

Doubt

PHOOF! We shot into the Whitney Pond.

Ace and Finnegan sat there by themselves.

Ace looked at me smiling then said, "AHHH! I thought you were dead."

"I'm not dead," I said. I just needed some time to think."

"Not you," said Ace. "You!" He pointed at Nereid. "I saw you blast off." Ace swam up to Nereid and said, "This is all your fault! You wouldn't let us tell you what happened that night you caught us sneaking out." Ace gave me a nasty look and said, "Why did you bring him here?"

Before I could answer, Nereid said, "Caulder or Ace if you prefer, I owe you an apology. I'm sorry. I was wrong. I should have listened to you that night."

Ace said, "Apology accepted," shaking Nereid's hand. "Blaze, where's your earpiece? I tried talking to you. I thought you got gobbled up by one of those fish things."

I reached in my pocket pulling out the ear gadget. I put it in my ear, turning it on.

"What is going on down there?" I heard. "Someone tell me something. Ace, were you just talking to Blaze? Is he okay?" It was William R. Whitney IV. "Blaze, are you down there?"

I had to smile. It sounded like William was worried about me. I answered him, "Yes, William, I'm here and I'm okay."

William said, "I have a Tritonan update."

I said, "Hold on a minute, William. We have

a new member to the group." I reached in my other pocket pulling out Arianna's ear gadget. I handed it to Nereid and said, "Put this in your ear. Now you will be able to hear and talk with us and William."

Nereid reached up fumbling with the little ear gadget until it disappeared in his extra large ears.

"Who is the new member?" asked William.

Nereid responded, "My name is Nereid. I am an Elder from the Neptune Training Academy."

"Awesome," said William. "GG's journal said the Elders eventually become the Ancients who rule over their home moons."

Nereid put his head down and sighed.

I forgot Nereid wouldn't be able to become an Ancient of his home moon if he is stuck on Earth.

William said, "According to this journal, the meetings take place on the morning of the full moon, not at night. You have around twelve hours to rest up before the meeting."

Nereid seemed to come back to reality. He

said, "We can go to the Whitney Observatory until the meeting? You have some training to do with Ace and Finnegan and I need to get a look at that prophecy."

Ace pointed to himself and silently mouthed, "With me?"

William butted in, "I'll meet you all at the edge of the pond and give you a lift to the observatory. Blaze, warn Nereid about Butler. William, over and out."

Finnegan jumped up from the pond bottom, faced Nereid, saluted, and said, "At your service, Sir."

Nereid said, "At ease, Finnegan."

While we waited for William to arrive, I filled Nereid in on GG, William, and Butler.

"What is that?" asked Nereid.

I said, "That is William in his NASA Apollo 17 Space Suit."

WOOF, WOOF, Butler ran up to Nereid. He

opened his mouth and Nereid disappeared. Butler looked around for him. Nereid reappeared next to me.

Nereid said, "That Butler almost ate me."

We all laughed.

I said, "He only wanted to lick you."

William knelt down in his clunky space suit in front of Nereid holding out his oversized space gloved hand. "Hi, I'm William R. Whitney the fourth, the great grandson of William R. Whitney. Pleased to meet you."

We climbed into the same container used earlier, except this time without the lid. We headed to the observatory.

When we came to the top of the stairs inside the observatory, Nereid looked around and said, "This is like a large version of the Cosmic Compound."

Nereid walked over to me and said quietly, "Start practicing your fire rings on Ace while I get a look at the Prophecy."

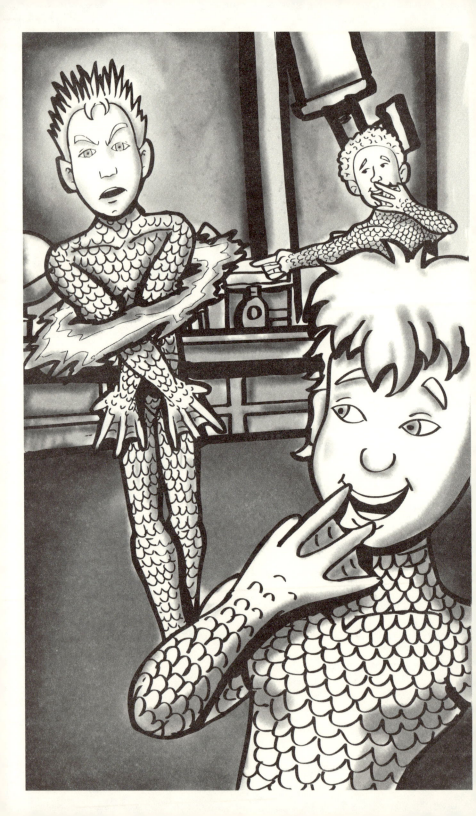

"No way," I said. "What if I hurt him?"

"You won't hurt him. This is your training. Now do it," ordered Nereid.

Ace and Finnegan didn't seem to know what was going on. I felt my stomach do somersaults. Nereid had a point. I needed to know if I could imprison a Pond Punkie.

I turned away from Ace and blew a fire ring.

He must have seen it because he said, "Cool, Blaze, I knew you were the chosen one."

I raised my arms aiming them at the ring, and said, "To the Power of Neptune." It worked. The ring stopped in place. I guided it to Ace, slipping it around him. The fire ring slid down to his waist locking his arms by his sides.

Ace twisted his hands so his palms faced upward. He shot out some water from his hands breaking the fire ring.

"What was that all about!" shouted Ace. He ran up to me butting his chest against mine.

Flames escaped out of Finnegan's nose. At least someone thought it was funny.

I said, "It was Nereid's idea. I only did what he said." I backed away from Ace.

Nereid spoke up, "The prophecy speaks of a chosen one with a fire ring in his hand. Those fire rings are imprisonment rings. Blaze has this special ability because he is a Larissan twin. These rings won't hurt you."

Nereid went on explaining to Finnegan and Ace how I needed to practice on them.

"No way! No way at all! Not on me again. If he needs practice, let it be on you," said Ace.

Finnegan saluted me and said, "At your service. Give it a try on me."

I puckered up, blew out a ring guiding it at Finny. It hung over his head for a bit until I brought it down. It locked his arms inside the ring like Ace.

Finny laughed, flames shot out of his nostrils breaking the ring. Why did it paralyze the fish and not these guys?

I said, "This is never going to work on the Tritonans. Finnegan can even get out of my so called imprisonment rings."

CHAPTER TWELVE

Practice Makes Perfect

"Blaze, can you blow more than one ring at a time?" asked William.

I said, "Sure, back home I would sit out by . . ." I noticed Nereid watching me. "Well," I said, "Ace and I used to sneak around getting gooey stuff for his punkie gel. While I waited for him to fill his tubes, I would see how many fire rings I could blow."

Nereid asked, "How come you never told anyone about this?"

"Because I thought it was a defect, like Finnegan and his flames coming out of his gills and nostrils. So Ace and I kept it our secret."

Nereid said, "The Ancients told the Elders of these imprisonment rings and of the ice slivers used on Arianna. Maybe you do need more than one ring to imprison a Pond Punkie. Try it on Finnegan again using more rings."

"Finnegan, are you okay with that?" I asked.

"At your service," he saluted grinning ear to ear.

I inhaled deeply, forming my mouth in a circle, and exhaled. Three fire rings came out drifting upward. I pushed my arms out, opening my palms, and said, "To the Power of Neptune." All three imprisonment rings stopped, hovering over his head. I lowered them down around his waist.

Finnegan didn't move. No flames shot out of his nose. He didn't blink.

Ace walked over to Finnegan poking him, and my force field sent Ace flying backwards landing on his butt.

"Hey! Who did that?" said Ace as he got back to his feet.

I hooted and said, "Welcome to my force field."

"Your what?" asked Ace.

"Go ahead," I said. "Try to touch Finny again."

"No way!" shouted Ace.

I walked up to Finnegan touching him. Nothing happened to me. Finny looked like the fish statue, frozen in place.

"I did it," I said. "It really works."

"Blazedale," said Nereid. "Free him with the flaming arrow."

"What if the arrow hurts Finny?"

Nereid said, "According to the Ancients, if the arrow connects with a ring, it shouldn't cause any harm."

"Alright, I'll give it a try," I said. "Ace, get ready in case I set Finny on fire. You can put him out." I raised my shaking arms aiming at Finny. I said, "I'm sorry, Finny, and To the Power of Neptune." I concentrated on the arrow shooting out of my hand

and directed it at Finnegan. It sailed through the air striking the middle fire ring. Finnegan collapsed on the desk.

We all ran up to him.

I said, "Finny, are you okay. I'm sorry. Please be okay."

"I'm alive," said Finny and "I am no longer at your service, Blaze!"

I slapped him on the back laughing and said, "I'm okay with that, Finny. I still have Ace to practice on."

Nereid said, "Blazedale, continue to practice and try capturing a moving target. I need to go over this prophecy with William."

I looked at Ace, smiling.

"Oh no you don't," he said taking off running.

"Perfect," I said. "A moving target."

PHOOF! I shot out three rings and had them zigzagging all over the place chasing Ace. He stopped to turn around and the three rings dropped down around him.

"Gotcha!" I cheered. Ace was imprisoned.

Flames shot non-stop out of Finny's nose. He guffawed and guffawed about Ace.

"Perfect," I said, imprisoning Finny too. This got easier and easier. I left them like that for a few minutes before freeing them with arrows. Neither one fell down. They both stood there.

I wondered if I could imprison two Pond Punkies at once. I inhaled deeply and concentrated on blowing out one fire ring after the other until I had six.

Ace and Finnegan ran in different directions. I raised my arms, speaking the words of our ancients, aiming one hand at Ace and the other at Finnegan. I steadied the rings over Finnegan, lowering them on him. The other three rings hovered in the air waiting for my command.

I saw Ace hiding behind one of those talking boxes on the desk. I guided the rings over his head lowering them over him. Ace tried to fight them off.

The rings imprisoned him leaving his arms stuck straight up in the air.

I heard clapping behind me. It was William and Nereid.

"Very good," said Nereid. "I think you have trained enough for one night."

"Thanks, Nereid. I'll release them now." I raised my arms, aiming one at Finny and the other at Ace. I wanted to see if I could shoot a flaming arrow out of each hand. I said, "To the Power of Neptune." A flaming arrow shot out of my left hand colliding with Ace's middle fire ring. Nothing came out of the right hand. I had to do it all again to free Finny.

Nereid walked over saying, "We should rest for a few hours. In the morning, we will plan our attack against the Tritonans based upon how many show up at the meeting.

I hoped my dad showed up at the meeting. I couldn't wait to show him what I could do.

Nereid asked, "Did you three figure out the water plants are edible and quite delicious?"

"Oh yeah," said Finnegan. "Ace and I tried out several plants while we waited for Blaze to return."

I said, "I haven't eaten and I'm starving."

William said, "I'll get you some water plants, Blaze. I need to check in with my mom letting her know Butler and I are staying the night in the observatory." William walked to the stairs and said, "Come on, boy. Come on Butler."

Ace walked over saying, "If you imprison me once more, we're no longer friends. Got it?"

"Got it," I said crossing my webbed fingers behind me.

Finny said, "Double what Ace said."

I held up my hand extending all three fingers and my thumb. Ace and Finnegan did the same with their hands. We all said, "Web Four."

I heard William clunking up the stairs. Didn't he ever take that space suit off? He handed me some stringy green vegetation. I took it cramming it in my mouth. "Mmmmmm, this is good," I said.

William laid out some soft fabric and said we could sleep on it. He then rolled out a bigger piece of fabric on the floor for himself. He called it a sleeping bag. Butler curled up next to him.

I lay there with visions of my dad in my head. I thought about Ember hoping she was on Neptune. I wished that prophecy was wrong and that both fire twins didn't land here. I drifted off to sleep.

CHAPTER THIRTEEN

Blue Moon Meeting

BEEP, BEEP, BEEP, BEEP . . . I heard William's beeper thing. I opened my eyes. It was light outside again. I could get used to this. It was always darker on Neptune.

Nereid went to the edge of the desk and asked, "What's happening, William?"

William replied, "The Tritonans have it snowing in Florida. It started out raining, but turned to snow not far from Lake Mary where Blaze thawed the cat. It's never snowed in Central Florida. It's all over the news."

Nereid said, "Good, at least we know where they are." He then started to give orders. "Everyone needs to wear GG's ear gadget. William, you should stay down by the pond in case anyone shows up after we leave for the full moon meeting."

"Okay and web four," said William as he held up his hand with his pinky finger folded down in his palm and the other three fingers and thumb up. "GG's journal said this means go in peace."

Nereid said, "Yes, it does." He held up his hand, stretched his fingers out to show his webbing, and said, "Web four to you, too, William."

I said, "This way, Nereid," walking over to the book Arianna pulled back yesterday. It seemed so long ago. I wished that sick feeling in my stomach would go away. I pulled the book back and dove in.

We landed in the pond near the tunnel entrance. One of those scary fish creatures was ready to eat us!

We backstroked as fast as we could. I aimed my hands and got ready to torch him when he turned into a Proteusan Pond Punkie.

Ace grinned and said, "Must be related to Bob."

The Proteusan held out his webbed hand to take mine and said, "Hi, the name is Devin, but my friends call me Shifty."

I shook his hand and saw myself looking back at me. I jerked my hand back. Devin chuckled, reappearing as himself. This punkie was a master at shape changing.

He said, "You should have seen your face. What did you say your name was?"

"I didn't." I said.

Nereid stepped in between the two of us extending his hand to Devin and said, "I am Nereid, the Elder of the Nereidan Clan."

Devin took his hand, but didn't shape shift this time. He went on to say, "Arianna should be here soon. I like to scare her when she comes out of the chute. However, I must say she has come to expect it. Still, I love to hear her laugh and see that twinkle in her eye."

Nereid said, "I have bad news, Devin."

"Please call me Shifty. All my friends do."

"Okay, Shifty. Arianna has gone from here. She came under an ice sliver attack from a Tritonan."

Shifty said, "Then the rumors are true. The Tritonans are here to take over Earth. Is it so, Nereid?"

"I'm afraid it is."

More Pond Punkies started to exit the tunnel. I kept an eye out for my dad. They swam through the leafy green plant that hid the opening and gathered around a circle of rocks. We now totaled eleven. It was cool to see the older Pond Punkies from all the different clans.

All talking stopped when the next punkie swam through the plant. It was a Tritonan. Her long, kinky, white hair trailed behind her. She stopped swimming and stood very still except for one thing. She rubbed the webbing between her fingers and I

realized it was Krystal. I looked around for Ember, but didn't see her.

"Blaze!" Krystal screamed, swimming towards me. We hugged and I heard muttering among the others. "What is a Tritonan doing here? We should take care of her now before she tells the others where we are. We are no longer safe here."

I asked her, "Where is Ember? Is she here on Earth?"

Krystal said softly, "Blaze, a smaller geyser went off under us when we tried to escape the crater. I ended up here and I don't know what happened to Ember. I'm sorry."

I held her hands and said, "Its okay. I'm sure she's safe." In my heart, I wasn't sure at all.

I turned to face the group and said, "This is Krystal. She is a Tritonan, but she is on our side." I tried to sound as convincing as I could.

One shouted, "She's a spy!"

Another one shouted, "Let's get rid of her now!"

Someone else said, "She can't be trusted!"

A Thalassan Pond Punkie spoke up. He looked more capable of being the chosen one than I did. His scales inflated with muscles all over his four-inch body. His yellow hair looked fuller and thicker than my red-headed mop. His yellow eyes pierced my eyes when he said, "Let's see if she can be trusted."

He turned and faced Krystal.

She started trembling.

The Thalassan said, "She is telling the truth, but I feel there is something hidden."

The Thalassan used his powers to read Krystal's mind. Thalassans are mind readers, but must be close to you in order to use their powers.

"STOP!" came from the back of the circle. It was Nereid. "We have very little time. I feel she can be trusted. The Tritonans are freezing Earth right now. Just like the Prophecy said they would."

Krystal squeezed my hands and whispered, "The Prophecy. What is he talking about?"

I said, "I'll explain later."

Nereid went on, "We must work quickly as a team to stop the Tritonans. They plan to take over this planet, and destroy our home moons."

The other punkies kicked up a fuss until this cute blue-eyed, blue-haired Naiadan swam right up to Nereid and said, "I am Nixie from the Naiadan Clan. What's this Prophecy you speak of?"

Nereid explained the Prophecy to everyone. When he got to the part about me being the chosen one, everyone stared at me.

He said, "It is true, Blazedale is the fire twin with the power of fire rings."

Nereid shared everything William told him about the Tritonans and went over a detailed plan of attack. Everyone had a role to fill.

Nereid said, "The key is to take out the Tritonans until we get to Kroiser. Blazedale, every time a Tritonan is caught off guard; you will put a fire ring around him."

Nereid answered a few questions, and we headed to the tunnel entrance.

I wished my dad was by my side. I hoped he was okay.

As we were about to enter the tunnel opening to leave on the mission, Greyson, a Galatean with black-as-night hair, turned to Krystal and said, "You will stay here. We have no use for your help."

Nereid swam up to Krystal and said, "Krystal, we could use your help here. If anyone shows up after we leave send them to Lake Mary. Would you do that?"

Krystal nodded, "If you say so, Nereid."

I told her, "We'll be back before you know it."

Krystal frantically rubbed the webbing between her fingers. Pieces of webbing dangled from her hand. By the time we got back, she might not have any webbing left!

Just before we entered the tunnel, Ace shouted, "Let's kick some Tritonan butt!"

The muscular Thalassan said, "I'll blast them right back to Neptune!"

Greyson, the Galatean watching Krystal said,

Milton, they will take one look at you and run."

Ace and I looked at each other and mouthed Milton. We both buckled over in laughter. When I lifted my head, Milton stood in front of me.

He asked, "You don't like my name?" pushing his powerful chest into mine, bumping me backwards.

I couldn't think of what to say, so I said what came to my mind first. "Milton is a lovely name."

The whole group exploded in fits of laughter including Milton.

I saw bubbles behind Finnegan rise up to the surface.

Ace said, "Finnegan, you better not start shooting flames out of your butt with that punkie gas!"

That was all it took. Flames shot out of Finnegan's nose. Everyone gazed at him.

Finnegan said, "I . . . I'm . . . okay Ace. I'm just a little nervous." PLOP. PLOP. More punkie gas bubbles floated to the surface and everyone laughed again.

Ace swam by and said, "Nice one, lovely name?"

Ace and I found our place in line following the others into the tunnel system.

SWOOSH! I loved that sound. We dared to fulfill the prophecy.

CHAPTER FOURTEEN

Chilled

We whizzed through the tunnels. I sped faster darting past Nereid. I thrust my hands in front of me shooting red flames at the ice making an opening for us to enter the lake.

Nereid swam up to me and said, "Great work. Now you are acting more like the chosen one."

I started to like the sound of being the chosen one. Now to get the job done.

The others shot out of the tunnel.

Finnegan and I raised our arms saying the words

of our Ancients, "To the Power of Neptune." Flames burst out melting the ice.

Finny mumbled something and nice size flames kept exploding out of his hands. The frozen lake soon gave way to liquid.

Nereid said, "Stick to the plan and be careful."

Ace jetted over to me and said, "Come on Blaze, this is our chance to show Kroiser who really rules! I knew all along that you were the chosen one."

I gave him the *yeah right look* and said, "Okay Ace, as you would say, let's go kick some Tritonan butt!"

All of us paused at the surface. It was dark now, more like being back on Neptune. Snow whipped all around our faces. This was good. The humans wouldn't see us. I didn't see anyone.

Greyson said, "Over there. Look to our right by that tall frozen palm tree. See it on the shore?"

We all said, "Yes."

Greyson said, "It's safe to exit there."

Nereid said, "Good eye, Greyson."

We went under water following Greyson to the shore. It was cold and comforting, just like home.

At the shore, Nereid took the lead and said, "Follow behind me, always touching the punkie in front of you." He crawled out of the lake.

Milton was in front of me. He touched Nereid and disappeared.

I felt his muscles ripple from my touch. Maybe Greyson was right. Kroiser would take one look at Milton and run. Nah, I thought Kroiser was just like Milton, not afraid of anyone.

I turned to see a Despinan Punkie disappearing as he touched my back. As if by magic, next to vanish was Nixie and behind her Ace. He gave me a nod before he vanished. The last to fade away was Shifty, the shape shifter.

It was hard to walk without bumping into Milton. I couldn't see how fast he was moving. After several bumps, we got a rhythm going and moved along smoothly.

Nereid said, "Stop here."

I heard Kroiser before seeing him.

"Paralyze them with the snow. Freeze anyone who gets in the way!" he shouted, standing on top of a frozen human, with his back to us. His arms aimed at the sky changing rain to snow. My scales stood on end.

Tritonans shielded him from the back and sides. I wondered if he knew about the Prophecy. Was he protecting himself from the fire rings?

Humans and their pets littered the ground covered with snow. Maybe the humans crushed a few Tritonans on their way down.

We charged into action. Ace and Nixie raised up two walls of water.

Devin and the others touched Nereid and vanished.

Finny and I came up behind the water wall.

I blew a few fire rings and got them ready to imprison a Tritonan.

Ace and Nixie flung the wall of water at the Tritonan behind Kroiser. He reacted quickly and froze it. I dropped the three imprisonment rings over his raised arms and held him. One down.

Milton shot out of thin air, body slamming the Tritonan to the right of Kroiser. He vanished as quickly as he appeared. Nereid must have been running beside him. I blew out some fire rings, shouting, "To the Power of Neptune," and waited for the Tritonan to get up. I sent the rings closer. The Tritonan stood up looking for what hit him. I had my opening. I whipped the rings around him. Two down.

Ace crawled next to me and said, "I think we can sneak up in back of Kroiser. I'll make a diversion and you imprison him." Ace crept towards Kroiser's back. The big bully didn't see us coming from behind.

I caught up with him and said, "Please don't tell me this is another one of your plans." Ace flashed me that crazy grin and I knew this wasn't a good idea.

We inched closer. Nixie slammed a small

hurricane into a Tritonan. She would expect me to imprison him. I blew out some fire rings, raised my arms, and said quietly, "To the Power of Neptune." I guided the fire rings toward the wet Tritonan and trapped him. Three down.

Kroiser turned around. Our eyes met! He sprayed me with ice. I felt my body start to freeze. I couldn't move anything. Where was Ace? I heard Kroiser roar with laughter. Everything faded away.

CHAPTER FIFTEEN

The Plan

"Blazedale" Someone called my name. My body felt warm again. "Blazedale, come on, be brave son," the voice said. My dad used to say that to me.

I opened my eyes and saw a reflection of myself, but older. It was my dad! His eyes filled with tears, but a smile stretched across his face.

I reached up squeezing my dad as hard as I could. He jerked a little and said, "Owww!" Then he squeezed me as if he was never going to let go.

"Are you okay, Dad? You're hurt."

"Blazedale, I'm supposed to be asking you if you're okay."

"I'm okay now that I found you." I clutched my dad tightly and it felt great.

I looked around for Ace. I didn't see him anywhere. We were behind a tree.

"Where's Ace? Is he okay? Did we stop Kroiser? When did you get here?" I had a ton of questions and couldn't get them out fast enough.

My dad said, "Whoa! Slow down, Tiger."

"Where's Ace?" I asked again.

My dad tipped my chin up so I looked into his fiery red eyes and said, "Kroiser froze Ace right after he froze you. Devin saw all of this happening and shape shifted into a Tritonan. He got you off the battlefield and went back for Ace. Kroiser realized what he was up to and slid Ace next to him. Kroiser said if we didn't retreat he would shoot deadly ice slivers into Ace."

I couldn't believe it. We came this far just to have Kroiser win.

"Are you okay?" asked my dad.

"No, not really," I said.

"Blazedale, everyone needs your help. Nixie filled me in on the plan. You need to try again. Don't worry, this time I'm right behind you." My dad helped me to my feet.

Then it hit me like a ton of ice. My dad was the one in the prophecy. He was the one more to even the score. He was the one to watch the fire twin's back as the battle soars. I felt like I could put twenty fire rings around Kroiser. Then I remembered Arianna.

"Dad," I said, "I can't. Kroiser is too powerful. He might use those deadly ice slivers. He said Elder Triton was training him to do something to you if he saw you on Earth. What if he kills you?"

"Blazedale, we're a team you and I. No one is going to kill us. At least not today," said my dad smiling at me.

"Dad, I have an idea."

My dad lifted me up, and said, "That's my son. What's the plan?"

"Where is Nixie?" I asked.

"Over there by that frozen palm tree." He pointed to our right where Nixie was peeking around the side of the frozen tree.

I signaled her to stay there. My dad and I made our way over to Nixie and found Finnegan with her.

Nixie said, "We're not sure what to do, Blaze. Every time we stop them, they just get back up because we can't imprison them."

"Nixie, Finnegan," I said. "Let's go ahead with the same plan. Nereid and the others are still out there. I can't communicate with them. My ear gadget won't work. I'm sure they saw Ace frozen next to Kroiser."

I asked my dad, "How long has Ace been frozen?"

He said, "The same as you. Nixie told me Kroiser

froze you for just a moment before I got here. Your friend Finnegan tried to thaw you, but got too nervous and for some reason could only shoot sparks out of his nose."

"He does that sometimes," I said.

Finnegan stood away from us staring at the ground. I walked up to Finny putting my hands on his shoulders, and said, "Finnegan, It's okay. You did great today. Come on, we have work to do. We have three more to go. Are you with me?"

Finnegan looked up, saluted me, and said, "At your service, Blaze."

"Alright!" I shouted.

"Is your ear gadget working?" I asked.

Finny looked down again and said, "I lost it."

"Don't worry about it. We'll be okay without it," I said. "Now I need you to take Ace's place and surprise the Tritonan by Kroiser with some heat so I can get some fire rings around him." Finnegan looked down again.

"Hey, Finny," I said. "You can do this. I know

that lately you've been mumbling something to yourself when you're using your powers and somehow it helps you blast awesome flames. Just keep mumbling the same thing." I gave him a friendly shove.

"Nixie," I said. "You wash out the Tritonan to Kroiser's right."

"Dad, you take out Slate. He's the one protecting Kroiser's back."

"Got it," said my dad.

"Everyone, listen up," I said. "I don't want to count on Nereid and the others since we lost contact with them. In order for this to work, speed and surprise is our only hope to save Ace. We can't give Kroiser time to think."

My dad said, "Okay, everyone, hands on top of mine." He shoved his hand out in front of his chest and all three of us placed our hands on top of his. My dad said, "TO THE POWER OF NEPTUNE!" We all repeated, "TO THE POWER OF NEPTUNE!" We pulled our hands away and set out on our mission to save Ace, Earth, Neptune and all its moons.

Nixie didn't waste any time. She had a wall of water headed toward one of the Tritonans before I had my fire rings ready. I inhaled as deep as I could. I exhaled along with eight fire rings. Eight wasn't enough! That's one fire ring short to imprison three Tritonans!

I thrust my arms out saying those powerful five words, "To the Power of Neptune." I shot three of the eight fire rings around the Tritonan Nixie attacked.

Finnegan got his flames back. He shot one right at a Tritonan. The Tritonan attacked it with freeze. When the two met, water splashed to the ground. That was just enough distraction. I guided three more fire rings to the Tritonan and encircled him. I only had two left.

It was up to my dad now. Kroiser didn't seem to notice his protected ring disappearing. Nereid popped out of nowhere in front of Kroiser. Kroiser shot ice at him, but Nereid vanished and popped

up in another spot. Kroiser didn't seem interested in killing Ace when he had an Elder as a new target. Way to go Nereid.

My dad was awesome. He shot the biggest flame I ever saw at Slate. The flame knocked him on his butt. I steadied the last two fire rings with my hands sending them toward my dad. Slate got to his feet and was ready to attack. I dropped the fire rings around him before he lifted his arms. My dad gave me a smile and a web four. I hoped those two rings were enough to hold him.

I inhaled several times. I knew this was it. I had to imprison Kroiser from behind before he decided to shoot Ace with the deadly ice slivers. Nereid vanished. Kroiser turned around. His eyes lit up with a white frost.

"Blaaaaaaaaaaaze!" he shouted. "I was saving this for your friend here, but I have had enough of you!"

"Bring it on, Kroiser," I shouted back exhaling three awesome fire rings.

Kroiser and I thrust our arms out in front of us. At the same time we both roared, "To the Power of Neptune!"

I threw my fire rings at Kroiser's head the same time his palms emitted shards of jagged ice slivers.

The first fire ring encircled Kroiser's head just as Finnegan's body flew out in front of me. Most of the ice slivers speared him. I felt some of the jagged slivers penetrate my scales.

"OWWWWW!" Pain shot through me as they entered my body. I glanced at Kroiser to see the next ring slip over his head. I hoped they would hold him. Finny why? Why would you do that? I reached down to pull an ice sliver out of my stomach and collapsed.

CHAPTER SIXTEEN

Resting Place

I heard a faint voice in my head. "Son, wake up. Come on Blazedale, talk to me." It sounded like my dad.

"Dad," I groaned. My dad gathered me tight to his chest. I could have stayed like that forever, but I had to know.

"Dad, is Finnegan dead? He jumped in front of me. He took all those ice slivers. Why? Why did he do that?"

My dad said, "He did that to save your life and give you time to imprison Kroiser. Nereid said Finnegan fulfilled a verse in the Prophecy."

I thought about that for a minute. I was wrong it wasn't my dad. Finnegan was the one to protect the fire twin's back as the battle soared.

"Is he okay?" I asked.

My dad said, "Nereid was quick to remove the slivers from him and I warmed him the best I could. He is hurt pretty bad and will need quite some time to heal. He should survive. Milton and Greyson took Finnegan back to the Whitney Observatory."

I felt so weak. I asked, "Will I die from the slivers? I don't feel so good right now, and I have so much to tell you."

Nereid leaned over my dad and said, "Blazedale, you will live to see another day. A few ice slivers hit you. Your father removed them and warmed you before they could do any real harm. You will be sore for a few days, but you are better off than Finnegan. What a courageous thing that Larissan did. And, you, Blazedale, prevailed over your doubts to fulfill the prophecy."

I nodded to Nereid and said, "Thanks for believing in me and helping me find my strength."

I turned back to my dad and asked, "How did you know where we were?"

He said, "I knew about the full moon meetings at the Whitney Pond. I arrived too late and was surprised to find Ember's friend Krystal. She filled me in on everything and here I am." He squeezed me again.

I asked, "Did we stop the Tritonans? Where..." I didn't get to finish my sentence because Ace knelt down by my side holding my hand up high with his and gave a web four. All the Pond Punkies gathered around me and did the same, shouting, "To the Power of Neptune!"

Black soot covered Ace's scales. He seemed to be oozing some punkie fluid, but other than that, he was the same old Ace. His spikes flopped over to one side on his head.

Ace said, "We stopped them. That jerk, Kroiser, actually froze us. He's stuck where you left him with the rings around him. To think what we could've done at the training academy if we knew you could imprison things." He gave me a light punch in the arm.

"Owww! Watch it," I said.

Ace just grinned, backing away.

Nereid said, "Blazedale, I noticed you only put two rings around one of the Tritonans. It seems to be holding, but you will need to add a fire ring to him to make sure he remains imprisoned."

My dad said, "Great job, Blazedale! I am so proud of you."

Nereid said, "Blazedale, I know you are weak and sore, but you have more work to do." He turned to face my dad and surprised me when they embraced. Then he said, "Brogan, I knew you were still alive. It is nice to see you again."

My dad said, "Thanks, Nereid. Great working with you again."

Working with you again, I thought. What was that about?

Nereid said, "Blazedale, because of your force field, you alone will need to move the imprisoned Tritonans to the bottom of the lake. They will stay there until we find a way back to Neptune."

"Do you think you can stand now?" asked my dad.

I got up and fell to my knees.

"Slow, not so fast," said my dad, helping me up.

I felt a little shaky. We walked over to the Tritonans. They looked freaky; frozen in place with different expressions on their faces. Kroiser still looked menacing even imprisoned in a fire ring.

My dad said, "It will be light soon."

I inhaled and it felt like someone punched me in the gut. I blew out a fire ring, raised my aching arms, and said, "To the Power of Neptune." I added the fire ring to Slate.

I grabbed an imprisoned Tritonan and slid him

on the frozen ground to the lake's edge. My dad reached up to help me and flew backwards. "Whoa! Forgot about that force field," said my dad.

It took all the strength I had to move seven of them. I grabbed them one at a time from the shore diving to the bottom of the lake. I placed them in thick water plants close to the tunnel opening.

Kroiser was the last one to move. I got the heebie jeebies when I held his stiff body transporting him to the bottom of the lake. I positioned him next to the others. He stared straight at me. I wondered if he knew what was going on. "YOU LOSE!" I yelled at him and swam back to the surface.

My dad asked me, "Do you know if they'll die down there?"

I said, "Nereid told me that anyone or anything imprisoned will be fine until I remove the imprisonment rings. He said no harm will come to them as long as the force field is protecting them."

My dad and I worked together as a team. First, we thawed the land and plant life. Nixie and Ace followed us around lifting the liquid from the thawed snow and flinging it into the lake. Next, we thawed the animals. The last thing we thawed was the humans.

All of us ran together toward the lake, diving in, and swimming to the tunnel opening.

Before we entered I said, "Dad, wait, I need to tell you something."

"What is it?" asked my dad.

"It's Ember. I can't feel her." I felt the emptiness inside of me where I should have felt Ember. "I don't know if she's on Earth or Neptune. I don't know if she's okay. I'm worried about her."

My dad asked, "Was she with you when the geyser erupted?"

"Yes and no," I said. "She was, but then she crawled to safety with Krystal."

My dad put his arm around my shoulder and said, "Well then, I'm sure she's safe on Neptune."

I looked up at him and said, "Dad, you saw

Krystal here on Earth and she doesn't know what happened to Ember."

My dad's gills looked to pulsate faster as he said, "Ember had the same training you did at the Academy and look at everything you did today. Let's see what we can find out back at the Whitney Observatory. Maybe one of the other Pond Punkies heard something about her. Maybe you will be able to communicate with her on Neptune. Don't worry, Blazedale; we won't stop until we find her."

Dive into another Pond Punkie adventure!

Turn the page for a glimpse of:

Pond Punkies

Book 2

~ Pocket Pals ~

CHAPTER ONE

Run! I had to hide before it spotted me. I squeezed into a crack on the rocky mountain face. I felt it getting closer. My body jerked from side to side with every step the creature took. Its foul odor stung my gills.

Don't move! Oh gosh, don't move. It can't see me if I don't move.

A glowing green eye stared at me through the crack. Its long hairy feelers explored my hiding place. Rows of jagged teeth peered from its mouth. Foamy spit dripped, pooling at my feet.

PRRRRR. The creature moaned, rubbing its head on the gray rock face. That is when I saw the resemblance.

I reached into my pockets. The pocket pals were gone!

NEPTUNE FACTS

- The planet is named after the Roman god of the sea, Neptune.
- Methane gas on Neptune absorbs red light and reflects a bluish green color into space.
- It is bitterly cold with temperatures reaching -360° Fahrenheit with violent winds reaching speeds over 700 miles per hour.
- If Neptune were hollow, it would hold sixty Earths.
- The Great Dark Spot did exist at one time on Neptune and may have been an Earth size storm.
- The Scooter is a white patch of clouds that lies deep in Neptune's atmosphere. The *Voyager* Scientists named it *The Scooter* because it scoots around the planet.
- Neptune has a set of four rings, which are narrow and very faint.
- Being the eighth planet from the sun, the brightest daylight on Neptune is like nightfall on Earth.

TRITON FACTS

- Neptune's largest moon is named after the Greek god of the sea's son, Triton.
- Triton orbits in the opposite direction of all the other moons and Neptune. If Triton had been born in orbit around Neptune, it would have moved in the same way as the planet's rotation. Therefore, it seems as though Triton was born as a separate world and *captured* by Neptune's gravity as it passed close by.
- Triton's surface is an icy landscape of frozen nitrogen.
- Triton is extremely cold at -397° Fahrenheit.
- Triton has active ice volcanoes that throw a mixture of nitrogen, methane, and other substances high above the frigid surface.
- Parts of Triton's surface resemble the texture of a cantaloupe melon.

Lisa Riebe's joy of children reading inspired her to write this fantasy and science fiction adventure. She lives in Illinois with her family.

Cynthia Nunn worked with her sister Lisa on writing this exciting adventure.

You can find out more about, the authors and Pond Punkies at **www.pondpunkies.com**

Eric Scott Fisher is a freelance illustrator living in Morris, Illinois with his wife Sarah and daughter Molly. He devotes his time illustrating books and magazines for children and young readers. Please visit his website at **www.ericscottfisher.net**

COMING SOON
Pond Punkie Trading Card Game

Jacket Illustration © 2009 By Lisa Riebe
Jacket Illustrated by Eric Scott Fisher

Ravine Publishing
100 W. Commercial
Suite 1C #158
Morris, IL 60450
Printed in the U.S.A.